Red Penguin and the
Missing Sushi

By Eileen Wacker • Illustrated by Alan M. Low

ISBN 978-0-9844207-3-5

Fujimini Island is home to many animals:

Pandas climb the
mountain slopes,

Penguins frolic on
the rocky shores,

Sea animals swim
in the glassy bay,

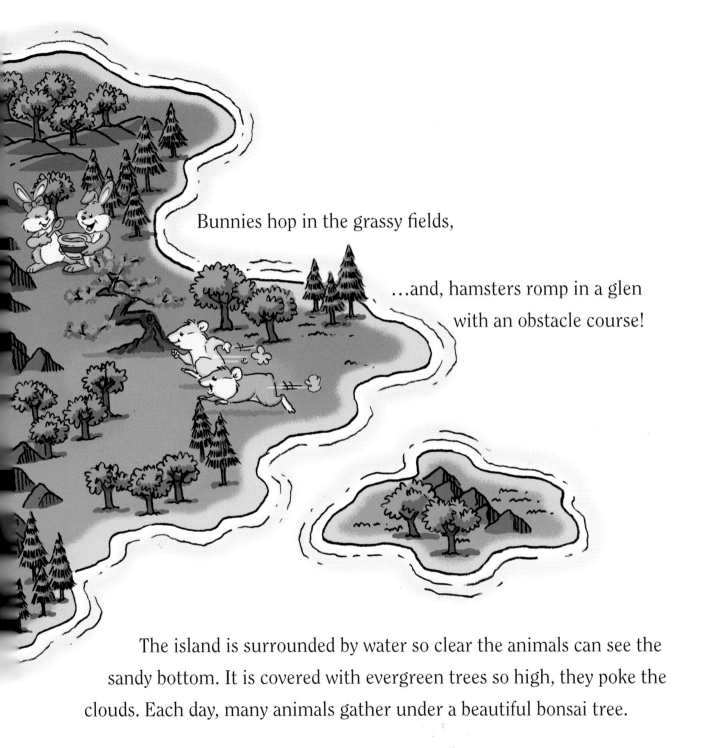

Bunnies hop in the grassy fields,

...and, hamsters romp in a glen with an obstacle course!

The island is surrounded by water so clear the animals can see the sandy bottom. It is covered with evergreen trees so high, they poke the clouds. Each day, many animals gather under a beautiful bonsai tree.

Today Red Penguin is going to the bonsai tree to meet other animal chefs. They will finish the menu for tonight's Moon Festival Celebration. As she leaves, the sea animals remind her to move the party to the water so they can join. She promises, "This year, we will celebrate the full moon in the bay and *everyone will be included!*"

Other parts of Fujimini Island are buzzing with excitement. In the glen, the hamsters are eager for the Moon Festival Celebration. They are making beautiful lanterns. Brown Hamster wonders where Pink and Green Hamster are as he leaves for the bonsai tree.

Under the bonsai tree, the head chefs gather and Brown Hamster reads the party list. "Okay, the pandas are making *dim sum* and noodles. Bunnies, you provide fruit and moon cakes. Penguins, you prepare the sushi. And we're bringing the salad. Is everyone okay with that?"

Green Hamster is spying with his best friend, Pink Hamster. "Every year we get stuck making boring salad," he whispers. "Everyone else makes colorful and fun dishes – it's NOT fair!"

Pink Hamster agrees, "And the bunnies make those beautiful treats that everyone says are the best! No one ever says salad is the best!"

Suddenly, Red Penguin starts bragging, "This is our best year ever. We have more than ten different kinds of sushi and everything is perfect. We are creating a work of art."

"What a show off!" Green Hamster huffs, but Red Penguin keeps talking. "Sushi is an art while salad is…well, just salad. I mean, it's nutritious and you might be able to make it pretty. Let me know if you hamsters need some advice."

Green Hamster says, "Let's go see what makes this sushi so special!" They scamper to the coast ahead of Red Penguin. She arrives and starts bossing everyone around – "More rice on that one…" and "Wrap that seaweed just a little more carefully."

Green Hamster says, "She needs to be much more humble. Let's play a little trick on her. Let's hide her sushi until tonight… in the shade so it doesn't spoil."

While the penguins swim and surf, Pink and Green Hamster sneak the sushi into a crate with ice. "Let's hide this in our glen," whispers Green Hamster.

"Okay," agrees Pink Hamster. But after lifting it, she says, "It's so heavy. Let's find some place closer. How about the shady spot in the bunny field?"

They leave the crate covered with banana leaves in the shade.

A few minutes later, Orange Bunny comes hopping into the field. She sees the crate and thinks, "I can cover this with a table cloth and it will be perfect for the sweets." She calls the bunnies to move the heavy crate to the bonsai tree for the party.

As the pandas are putting their *dim sum* in boxes, they hear the penguins squawking very loudly. "Hey down there, what's going on?" asks Black Panda to the frantic penguins.

Red Penguin is shouting, "The sushi is missing! Someone took the sushi!"

"We didn't touch the sushi," exclaim the confused penguins. "Then where is it?" she cries.

Since there is normally no shouting on Fujimini Island, everyone runs toward the bonsai tree to find wise Brown Hamster. "Our beautiful sushi is missing," sobs the Red Penguin. Everyone just stands there looking surprised.

13

Green and Pink Hamster look at each other. "Oh boy, we'd better go get the sushi." They take off running to the bunny field. When they get there, they discover the crate is GONE! "Oh no! Somebody *really* took the sushi! We need to find Brown Hamster," cry the two hamsters.

But meanwhile, Brown Hamster is out trying to find the sushi. He finds Blue Dolphin and says, "Excuse me, but we're missing some party sushi. Do you know anything about it?"

Blue Dolphin replies, "I don't know anything about the sushi, but I know we begged Red Penguin to move the party to the water. She promised she would, but we heard she forgot. Blue Whale is pretty upset about being left out of the Moon Festival Celebration again this year."

Brown Hamster calls out to the reclusive whale. "Hello, Blue Whale! Could I talk to you about some missing sushi?" Blue Whale shouts back, "I don't know anything about sushi and I want to go to the party!"

"Okay, but have you seen any sushi? Could you have swallowed it by mistake?" asks Brown Hamster.

"Why? Do you think that because I am so huge, I swallow things and do not even notice? I do NOT know anything about sushi and Red Penguin promised the party would be in the bay!" He sprays a torrent of water and swims away.

16

Brown Hamster walks back to Red Penguin and says, "Blue Whale is upset that the Moon Festival Celebration is not in the bay."

"Oh no!" cries Red Penguin, "He asked me to make tonight a water party so everyone can go. I forgot my promise because I was admiring my sushi. This whole thing is my fault."

Brown Hamster walks back and updates the other animals. "Blue Whale is upset and Red Penguin thinks everything is her fault. What a mess and we still can't find the sushi."

Green and Pink Hamster pull Brown Hamster aside. "Wise Brown Hamster, please help us. We took the sushi and hid it in the bunny field, but when we went back to get it, it was GONE. We didn't mean to cause trouble."

"What? But, why did you take the sushi? You don't even like sushi," says Brown Hamster.

"Well, Red Penguin was showing off about her sushi and we always get stuck making boring salad," they reply. "And now everyone is upset and the sushi is REALLY missing. We're sorry."

Brown Hamster says, "Well, she already feels bad about bragging. Let's go find her sushi. And by the way, everyone loves salad."

They rush to the bunny field. "Hello bunnies! Could we please talk to you about the missing sushi?"

The hamsters describe the crate and Orange Bunny exclaims, "Yes, we thought it would be a great table for tonight! It is under the bonsai tree. Now we know why it was so heavy."

Leaving the Bunny field, Brown Hamster says quietly, "When I asked Blue Whale about the sushi, I hurt his feelings. And, Red Penguin is pretty upset. This is supposed to be a fun celebration. What do you think we should do?"

Green Hamster offers, "We can bring our special lanterns from the glen to decorate a party boat. Then, we can sail out on the bay with a festival of lights. The sea animals will be really excited."

Brown Hamster replies, "That sounds like a great plan. Let's tell everyone we found the sushi and we're moving the party!"

The hamsters move the beautiful, colorful lanterns to make up for the sushi snatching. The pandas strengthen the boat so it is strong enough to hold the feast and the animals. Red Penguin is being nice by not bossing anyone around.

The animals ride out in the setting sun. The stars are shining and the lanterns burn brightly. "What a magical night. The food is delicious and the bay is beautiful," says Black Panda.

Blue Whale is swimming around them, spouting water. "I am so happy to be at

the party! And the beautiful sushi tastes wonderful. Can I come next time?"

"I'm so glad you are all here," says Red Penguin humbly, "we should hold the Moon Festival Celebration in the bay every year so everyone can join. You are much more important than sushi." Everyone agrees.

The animals glance one more time at the glowing moon. Then, yawning, they head home for a good night's sleep filled with dreams of good friends, water parties and a fabulous feast.

And Pink and Green Hamster make a pact never to hide anything again.